Dear Parent:
Your child's love of reading starts here!

Every child learns to read in a different way and at his or her own speed. Some go back and forth between reading levels and read favorite books again and again. Others read through each level in order. You can help your young reader improve and become more confident by encouraging his or her own interests and abilities. From books your child reads with you to the first books he or she reads alone, there are I Can Read Books for every stage of reading:

SHARED READING
Basic language, word repetition, and whimsical illustrations, ideal for sharing with your emergent reader

BEGINNING READING
Short sentences, familiar words, and simple concepts for children eager to read on their own

READING WITH HELP
Engaging stories, longer sentences, and language play for developing readers

READING ALONE
Complex plots, challenging vocabulary, and high-interest topics for the independent reader

ADVANCED READING
Short paragraphs, chapters, and exciting themes for the perfect bridge to chapter books

I Can Read Books have introduced children to the joy of reading since 1957. Featuring award-winning authors and illustrators and a fabulous cast of beloved characters, I Can Read Books set the standard for beginning readers.

A lifetime of discovery begins with the magical words "I Can Read!"

Visit www.icanread.com for information
on enriching your child's reading experience.

Adventures of
Pete the Cat

ISBN: 978-0-06-274204-9
Manufactured in Dong Guan City, China
Lot#:
19 20 21 SCP 5 4
07/19

Adventures of
Pete the Cat

by James Dean

HARPER

An Imprint of HarperCollins Publishers

TABLE OF CONTENTS

Pete the Cat

PETE'S BIG LUNCH

by James Dean

Here comes Pete!

It is lunchtime.

Pete is ready to eat.

What should Pete eat?

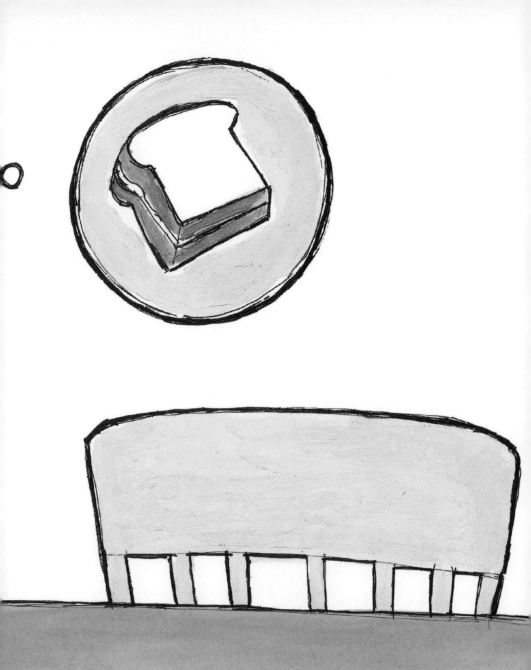

A sandwich would be nice.

Yes, Pete wants a sandwich.

Pete opens the fridge.

He takes out a loaf of bread.

He finds a yummy fish.

He adds tomato and mayo.

Pete looks at his sandwich.

It is too small.

Something is missing.

Pete knows what it needs.

His sandwich needs an apple.

Pete loves apples!

19

His sandwich needs crackers.

Crackers are crunchy.

Pete loves crunchy crackers!

Pete looks at his sandwich again.

It is still too small.

Pete is very hungry.

Pete adds a pickle.

Pete adds cheese.

Pete adds an egg,

two hot dogs,

a banana,

and a can of beans.

Something is missing.

Pete adds ice cream!

He takes three huge scoops.

Pete's sandwich
is too big
for Pete to eat.

Pete wonders
what to do.
Pete thinks
and thinks.

"I've got it!" Pete says.
Pete calls all of his friends.

He asks them to come over.

Everyone goes to Pete's house.
They are all very hungry.

Pete shows them
his big lunch.

"Are you hungry?" asks Pete.

Pete's sandwich is big enough for everyone.

"Dig in!" says Pete.

Pete's sandwich is good.

Pete's sandwich is VERY good.

Pete's sandwich is all gone.

Pete's friends are full.

They liked Pete's big lunch.

"Thanks for lunch,"
Pete's friends say.
"Thanks for sharing!"

"You're welcome," Pete says.
Sharing is cool.

Pete the Cat

PLAY BALL!

by James Dean

40

Here comes Pete the Cat.

Pete has a mitt.

He has a bat and a ball.

What will Pete do today?

Pete will play baseball!

Today is the big game.

The Rocks are playing the Rolls.

Pete and his team get set.

They play catch.

They take turns hitting.

It is time to play ball!

The Rocks bat first.
Pete waits for his turn.

Crack! The batter hits the ball.

He runs to first base.

"Way to go!" Pete cheers.

"Batter up!" says the umpire.
Pete goes up to bat.

The pitcher throws the ball.

Pete swings the bat.

He misses the ball.

Strike one!

The pitcher pitches again.

Pete swings too high.

Strike two!

The pitcher winds up.

He throws.

Pete strikes out.

But Pete is not sad.

He did his best.

Pete's friend Ben is up.

Ben hits a home run!

"Way to go!" cheers Pete.

The Rolls go up to bat.

The Rocks go to the field.

Crack! Here comes a fly ball!
"I've got it!" calls Pete.

The ball hits his mitt.

But Pete drops it.

He is not sad.

He did his best.

Another hit!
This time Pete catches it,
but he throws it too far.

Pete is up at bat again.

He wants to hit the ball.

The first pitch is too low.

Pete does not swing.

Ball one!

The next pitch is too high.

Pete does not swing.

Ball two!

The third pitch is inside.

The fourth pitch is outside.

Pete gets four balls.

Pete wanted to get a hit.

But a walk is cool, too.

The next batter gets a hit.

Pete runs as fast as he can.

Pete wants to score,

but he is out at home plate.

Pete is not sad.

He did his best.

The game is over.

The Rocks win six to three!

"Way to go!" calls Pete.

"Good game," the Rocks say.
"Good game," the Rolls say.

Pete did his best.

He had fun.

What a great game!

Pete the Cat
Pete at the Beach

By James Dean

It is a hot day!

Pete the Cat goes to the beach

with his mom and his brother, Bob.

"Let's go in the water,"
Bob says.

"Maybe later," says Pete.

Bob likes to surf.

He rides the big waves.

It looks like fun.

"I'm hot," says Pete.

"Go in the water," says Mom.

"Maybe later," says Pete.

73

Pete makes a sand castle.

His mom helps him dig.

Here comes a big wave.

And there goes Pete.

Oh, no!

Where did his sand castle go?

Bob rides a big wave.

"Wow!" says Pete.

"That looks like fun."

Pete and his mom take a walk.

They find seashells.

They see a crab.

Pete's feet get wet.

His feet feel cool.

The rest of him is hot.

It is time for lunch.

Pete eats a sandwich.

He drinks lemonade.

The sun is very hot.

And Pete is very, very hot.

Bob is wet and cool.

"Let's play ball," says Pete.

"No, thanks," says Bob.

"I want to surf."

Pete throws the ball.

His mom catches it.

"Let's get our feet wet,"
says Mom.
"Well, okay," says Pete.

The water is cool.

It feels good.

Pete goes in deeper.

Bob waves to Pete.
"I want to show you
how to surf!" he yells.

Pete does not say
"Maybe later."
He says, "Let's do it!"

"Lie on the board," says Bob.

Pete lies on the board.

"Paddle," says Bob.

Pete paddles out.

He waits for a big wave.

A big wave is coming!

"Stand up!" says Bob.

Pete stands up.

Then Pete falls down.

It was scary,

but it did not hurt.

"Try again later," says Bob.

Pete wants to try again now.

Pete lies down again.

He paddles out and waits.

Here comes a wave!

Pete stands up.

This time he rides the wave!

"Good job," says Bob.

Pete wants to surf all day.

Bob does, too.

So they take turns.

Pete and Bob rock and roll
with the waves.
What a great day!

It is okay to be afraid.

But it is more fun to surf!

Pete wants to look cool.

He asks everyone,

"What should I wear?"

"Wear your yellow shirt,"
his mom says.
"It is my favorite."

So Pete does.

"Wear your red shirt,"
Pete's friend Marty says.
"It is my favorite."

So Pete does.

"Wear your blue shirt,"
Pete's brother Bob says.
"It is my favorite."

So Pete does.

"Wear your long pants,"
Pete's teacher says.
"They are my favorite."

2+2=4

So Pete does.

"Wear the shorts with the fish,"
Pete's friend Callie says.
"They are my favorite."

So Pete does.

"Wear the polka-dot socks,"
the bus driver says.
"They are my favorite."

So Pete does.

"Wear the cowboy boots,"
Grumpy Toad says.
"They are my favorite."

So Pete does.

"Wear the tie with the stripes,"
Emma says.
"It is my favorite."

So Pete does.

"Wear your baseball hat,"
his coach says.
"It is my favorite."

So Pete does.

Pete puts on all the clothes.

Does he look cool?

121

No.

Pete looks silly.

He also feels very hot!

Pete goes home.

He changes his clothes.

Pete puts on HIS favorite shirt.

Pete puts on HIS favorite pants.

Pete puts on HIS favorite socks.

Pete puts on HIS favorite shoes.

Pete puts on his sunglasses.

Pete says, "Now I am COOL."

If you want to be cool,
just be you!